SPOOKY
SCARY

Anita Kirk

Published by Anita Kirk at Amazon

<u>Dedication</u>

Anita's most popular fan would be her father before he sadly got dementia, and he is now devastatingly blowing in the wind. Anita's family has supported her one hundred percent with her writing, and she thanks them for the encouragement and you for taking the time out of your day to pick her book up and read it.
If you do enjoy reading this book Anita would really appreciate a good review to show other people that you have enjoyed reading.

Acknowledgments

I would like to thank you for taking the time to pick this book out from the millions of books available out there to read, if you do enjoy reading this book your review would mean the world to Anita Kirk for her to enjoy reading and sharing this book with others on social media or in person would be most appreciated.
Thank you.

Contents

SPOOKY SCARY

Chapter Fifteen – Garlic Circle
Chapter Sixteen – Wind Circles

***SPOOKY SCARY* IS THE SAME AS *EROTICALLY SPOOKY*.**

THIS IS THE NO-ADULT CONTENT VERSION.

Scarborough and Whitby are in the United Kingdom, so you can visit these places in person and have fun visiting a unique and different place that you will never experience anywhere else in the world, Yorkshire is an amazing welcoming place full of friendly, chatty people with the Yorkshire Pudding being a favourite to eat.

Prologue

There is plenty of light humour inside of this story to keep you entertained.

Carlos gets woken by the television freezing in the same position with crows and the Devil on the screen with him freaking out, with him unable to get back to sleep going for a walk, he then notices what it looked like a witch floating in the air dressed in black.

Streetlights inside of the lampposts go dark with Carlos ending up in the graveyard, Witch Sue was holding a broomstick with a cauldron announcing that she was waiting for a blue stone falling from the sky to take over the world bringing dead bodies back to life, with her speaking gibberish making the weather turn for the worst.

Carlos, Pedro, and Olive are in danger when Witch Sue turns up at their door freezing their bodies making them unable to move with a disastrous raging fire taking over, with Witch Sue using her watch to assist her with a round dial containing a silver star.

Vampire soldiers with piercing black eyes take over with them out of control.

Attempts to trick and stop Witch Sue and the vampires were chaotic, with dangerous, unpredictable bloody situations waiting around every corner that they turn making their lives even more difficult, and you will never look at a hat in the same way again.

Helpful messages are left to warn people on a phone of the danger ahead, giving them useful advice that they should listen to, do they listen?

Under the Rumble factory in Sky, it is life-threatening, do they manage to avoid being bitten, or does the blue stone help?

Do they survive after crashing into the Scarborough Sea?

Do the bats, the broomstick, and the spiders pass on and communicate the information to the vampires?

Do the garlic circles help to protect the uninfected from the vampires?

Does the silver star on the watch and the lampposts change anything?

Is the dagger with the blue stone embedded inside of the handle the key to winning the battle causing an unexpected explosive effect?

You will enjoy reading to find out all of these answers with you chuckling along with the adult story, with it keeping your eyes glued to every page and you will want to share the story with your adult and younger family and friends, because wherever you are reading this book you will not be able to control your laughter.

SPOOKY SCARY

Chapter One

Graveyard

"Hello my name is Carlos, and I have decided to go for a walk in the middle of the dead of night because I can't sleep because mysteriously the television turned on when I was fast asleep on its own, with it startling and scaring me awake, I picked up the remote control from the dressing table pushing the off button numerous times with the red light flashing but it wouldn't turn off, it had crows and the Devil on the television screen frozen, it would not turn off for a while, but it did eventually and then the birds in the trees were tweeting an annoying tune loudly together and on top of all that it is too warm in my bedroom so I couldn't get back to sleep because I felt freaked out with it feeling very disturbing in my head, it has messed with my thoughts in a bad way, me and my family have recently moved here with our parents living in our Rumble family run meat business, it is a little bit uneven underfoot because of the muddy ground, I am struggling to stop myself from falling in this graveyard near to the graves, creepily I have just noticed my name on a gravestone, and the streetlights have just gone off, in my opinion, I think that we must be having a power cut!"

Carlos looked up at the sky. "It looks like there's a shooting star in the sky and there are bats with spiders on their backs flying around me, it feels like they are harassing me with me creepily hearing their wings flying so close to my face, so I am using my torch on my phone so that I can only just see where I am stepping, and I have just noticed an extra dark shadow of a person ahead that looks like a lady at a glance, it feels a bit eerily spooky with me just mainly hearing creepy bat wings, in my opinion, I think that she is a witch with a long black cloak floating around in the dark misty eerie graveyard field at the back of the houses near to my house because normal people don't look like that, I guess that it was a dead end for everyone here, this may be a surprise to you, but I am informing you that it is not halloween, so I really can't understand and get my head around this, why are you dressed like that with black bats flying around you with what it sounds like ultra sonic squeaks coming from them and it looks like there are spiders on the bats backs?"

The witch replied. "My name is Witch Sue, anytime soon this is the moment in time that my blue stone will finally take over the world with help from my spiders and bats assistants, I am thinking about bringing all of these dead bodies back to life to be part of my army to control this world using my portable cauldron attached to my black broomstick, I am going to put a spell on every lamppost so that if you go near to certain lampposts you will change into what is on the picture card on the lamppost and do you know why cemeteries have got walls and fences?"

Carlos sounded fed up laughing slightly. "Please stop speaking rubbish, you will be telling me that the shooting star that I noticed on my way here was the blue stone next, there is no chance anything like that could happen around here you are a crazy lady and I presume that they have got walls and fences to give a bit of privacy to the relatives and the other year my father got home finding me in front of a roaring fire, he wasn't very happy because we didn't even have a fireplace!"

Witch Sue giggled, saying a spell while stirring her black cauldron with her wooden spoon. "Dead bodies come to be my army and make the living do crazy things for our entertainment and cemeteries have got fences and walls because people are dying to get in and yes that shooting star was probably the blue stone getting closer to us!"

Carlos smirked, looking at her. "I don't know how you have done it, but the wind has suddenly started howling and torrential rain has started to pour down heavily onto the floor causing many large puddles for me to avoid stepping into, the puddles have turned icy, slippery under foot and icicles have started to dangle from the trees with the temperature suddenly dramatically dropping with me noticing the condensation droplets from our breath hovering into the air!"

Witch Sue looked at Carlos with an evil laugh. "This is nothing compared to what is coming to you and everyone around you because your world will be turned upside down, and you will never be the same again, and do you know what a fish is called with no eyes?"

Carlos sounded fed up and annoyed, raising his voice speaking. "I am going home if that is what you are planning to do causing trouble, you look scary with your dress being bulky at the bottom, and it is even stranger with all of these bats circulating around me with spiders sat on their back using it as a flying car to transport them, it feels like they are going to pounce on me, and I am unable to see your feet and what is a fish called with no eyes?"

Witch Sue muttered as Carlos walked off. "The answer is a fsh."

Carlos shouted back. "Oh yeah, that's a corny joke, and are these bats your only spooky friends with you being an official weirdo?"

Witch Sue cackled. "Yes, the bats and spiders are my friends, they will do anything for me, they would enjoy mainly attacking people like you and I would love watching them attack you with me getting plenty of enjoyment out of it!"

Chapter Two

Creepy

Carlos looked scared, and a little freaked out walking home mentioning to a few dog walkers that had walked past him to not go near to Witch Sue because she was seriously creepy, with them sounding curious walking towards her like they were drawn to her after being warned not to.

People walked near to Witch Sue in the graveyard saying. "We have been warned that we need to walk as far away from you as we can because I know that it is dark, but you look like you have lost the plot dressed in morbid, dark clothing with bats containing spiders on their backs flying around us!"

Carlos arrived home. "I am home now next to our Rumble meat factory, I just need to dry off, I think that I need to ignore that insane lady dressed up as a witch calling herself Witch Sue, but it was odd it turning into an icy cold creepy atmosphere when she turned up, the weather is normally quite mild, I live with my brother and sister Pedro and Olive in a poor town called Sky with us all in our forties, we do not have much money with our parents owning a meat company called Rumble with massive walk-in fridges inside of our large factory to keep everything cool to sell onto our customers!"

Carlos's father Mick shouted from the sofa, muttering. "I don't know what is wrong with the tap in your kitchen because it had creepily turned on without me touching it, then the water pipe burst under the sink and now the television has turned on without me touching it with crows and the Devil on the television screen and is it you that has just opened the front door, Carlos?"

Carlos smiled. "Yes, it is me. Thank you for cleaning all of the water up. What you have just said is giving me goosebumps on my arms. I can smell the cigarette smoke from my friend who died a while ago, and it is strange how a plant pot has just fallen off the shelf with no known reason!"

Mick sounded relieved. "It felt a bit creepy before you came in, please put the television on then we can watch the news now that I have finally got that rubbish off, I will help you clean the soil up later from the plant pot and, I don't know why crows and the Devil appeared on the television, we can now see what is going on in the world, and I can hear Olive and Pedro getting ready upstairs with the floorboards creaking, we must have been seeing things maybe, let's just not speak about this again!"

Carlos listened upstairs. "Olive and Pedro are still snoring, that is odd because I heard their footsteps as well, but there is nobody there and did you hear the door slam shut upstairs?"

Mick sounded puzzled. "How could I not hear the door and that's odd, they are up now, good morning, Olive and Pedro, the footstep sounds must have been in my imagination as well!"

Olive shouted downstairs, sounding puzzled. "Good morning and there was no reason for that door to slam, how strange!"

Carlos was distracted, looking up at the sky through the window. "That's the second time that the crows and the Devil were on the television, and I don't know why you have come to see me so early in the morning, I presume that you couldn't sleep either, look an item that was not rain has just fallen from the dark cold sky above making a large thud on the floor outside of our Rumble meat fridge a couple of doors away from here by the look of it and at least it is warmer here and I must have misread my name on the gravestone!"

Carlos's father Mick walked outside of the house muttering to himself loudly mentioning about the large walk-in fridge, saying that he would look for the item that had fallen from the sky while walking off towards the Rumble factory. "I was here to see you early because I couldn't sleep either noticing you walk past our window, I will go and investigate and come back to you Carlos, we will watch the news when I see you later and yes, it is impossible to have your name on a gravestone because you are not dead!"

Carlos walked outside of his home as Mick arrived back. "What did you find?"

Mick looked at his hand. "I have found the item that has fallen from the sky, and I am looking at it, it is a bright light blue stone about the size of a small apple, and I am admiring how pretty it is with it glimmering, I will hide it in the Rumble fridge for us to look at later!"

Carlos smiled. "I like the look of that light blue stone, it's so cool!"

Mick explained. "I will put it onto this fridge shelf, I am not sure what else to do with it and I am just thinking about a customer offering me a million pounds if I could reach the top shelf to get his beef without a ladder, I said that I couldn't do it because the steaks are too high!"

Carlos laughed. "You are funny, father!"

Mick mentioned that he would go home to Jo. "I will go and make Jo a coffee for when she wakes and put the local radio on so that she can wake up to calming music with a cuddle and a kiss from me with me gently stroking her hair until she wakes up properly and we can then enjoy listening to the presenters that behave like clowns that run the radio show, they make us laugh so much, especially when people phone in mentioning what they have been up to, it's better than putting the creepy television on!"

Carlos stood at the door for a minute, waving. "Yes, you are correct a listener the other day that was talking live on the radio admitted that they had forgotten their real age, and another listener admitted that they call their partner ninety-five percent because they hardly ever get anything one hundred percent correct!"

Mick laughed. "I remember that because we mentioned that we wished that we were a bit younger, and you get forgetful, I suppose, as you get older and no matter how much people think that they are the best at everything, nobody is perfect!"

Carlos waved even stronger. "See you later father, yes, I totally agree that they are funny on the radio, they make me laugh as well, look after my mother and only make her a coffee if she is awake and enjoy your comedian radio presenters!"

Mick arrived home speaking in a low tone. "I am home honey, are you awake Jo?"

There was no answer with Mick sitting down in his lounge.

Chapter Three

Spell

Back at Carlos's house.

Carlos sat down on the sofa. "Good morning, Olive and Pedro, I am just thinking the other day I walked into a petrol station store that I was buying milk from, my friend that drove me there got some petrol, and none of the petrol pumps worked so I asked the lady behind the counter if she had her pumps on and, the shopkeeper replied with. "No, I am wearing boots!"

Pedro laughed. "I can imagine that in my head, I am going to be giggling to myself most of the day now every time that I notice a pair of boots or pumps, and you need to iron that outfit for Olive that you offered to iron Carlos!"

Carlos was about to grab the iron. "I am glad that we are a close family with us always there to help each other with mother and father living next door to us, I am sure that I have just seen Witch Sue walk past the window with bats following behind her with spiders on their backs, she had better not come here, like my first words when I first started to talk as a child was oh dear, that's what I will say if she comes here with go away added on!"

Witch Sue knocked at Carlos, Olive and Pedro's door with Carlos answering their door as Sue pushed her way inside of their house. "What do you want, you are not coming in because I like it warm, I have just warmed up after what you did in the graveyard making it super cold and do you know what you call a cat on ice?"

Witch Sue walked into the lounge laughing, saying. "I will show my powers, and I will cast a spell on you all to kill you and is the answer a freezing cat!"

Carlos did not know what she was talking about. "Please just leave, I wish that I had never answered the door, you are getting on my nerves now, I am warning you that you are getting no response from me because I am too busy ironing Olive's clothes, you are not welcome here in our personal space and the answer is one cool cat!"

Pedro screamed. "I don't like the look of you, and where are your feet, you are obviously, in my opinion, a witch?"

Witch Sue ignored Pedro using her watch face on her arm with a torch coming from the watch shining it onto

Carlos's fingers, she then pointed the light at the ceiling with the light jumping around the room with it stopping Olive and Pedro's fingers from working as well with Carlos complaining. "My fingers have stopped working and I cannot hold the iron, and you are rude walking into our house, upsetting everyone in what was a calm atmosphere until you walked in!"

The iron dropped to the floor face down on the carpet with it immediately, causing a steamy cloud and an awful burning smell.

Pedro sounded upset. "We believe that you are a witch now, please let our fingers move again because our fingers are always the most reliable to count on!"

Witch Sue laughed, announcing. "You are funny Pedro, I have cast a spell onto yours, Carlos, and Olive's fingers stopping them from working temporarily, this has caused Carlos to drop the steaming hot iron onto the floor setting the carpet and the wooden floor on fire, I am showing you that I will always get my own way!"

Olive screeched with tears pouring down her face. "This is terrible watching the fire take hold and setting our house on fire, I am frightened for our lives because it is out of our control, we are going to be burnt to death, and it is getting extremely hot in here making us all sweat badly, and our skin is turning red as a beetroot!"

Carlos started to cry, begging Witch Sue. "Please stop what you are doing, you are ruining our lives, I don't want my name in the graveyard yet, I have too much to do in life, I can't die yet, and we are about to catch fire, we need a fire extinguisher, if we do live through all of this situation, a fire extinguisher is something that I will buy!"

Witch Sue left, leaving the house a burning inferno, looking a little upset and guilty shouting into their burning front door. "Don't worry because I will bring you back to life as a vampire when you have burnt to death before you get any chance of going to the morgue!"

Carlos, Pedro, and Olive could not get out of the house because Witch Sue had cast a spell on all of their fingers with fire taking over, with Pedro screaming. "We are not going to survive this amount of intense heat, it has set our house on fire with no help, and we are not able to open any doors to get out with them all having round handles because they are all melting and dripping on to the floor with the intense heat, I will burn my hands off if I attempt to get out, this is really upsetting me, it was nice knowing everyone and I love you all!"

Olive started to cry. "I have tried to break the window with no good results!"

Pedro screamed. "I can't avoid the flames anymore, let's have a group hug behind the door in the hope that someone will save us!"

Chapter Four

Piercing Eyes

The house fell silent, a day later Carlos's parents Jo and Mick walked into the front door of Carlos's burnt house with Jo struggling to speak with her choked up crying. "I think that it is sad that we are too late for us to save them, we need to call the fire brigade now to put out the rest of the flames, there isn't anything left to burn, I am surprised that there is still fire around us!"

Mick wiped tears from his eyes replying. "Look we have found Pedro, Carlos, and Olive dead behind the door with them previously unsuccessfully trying to get out by the way that they were positioned in the room together!

Jo had even more tears rolling down her face, replying. "I insist that we take Pedro, Carlos's and Olive's bodies to the Rumble meat fridge, I feel so distraught!"

Mick struggled to reply, sounding choked up. "I really want to know how this has happened, I wonder if it's anything to do with that light blue stone that fell from the sky, we will keep them instead of taking their bodies to a funeral director until they are buried!"

Jo had a red face with her being uncontrollably upset replying. "It won't be anything to do with a stone, I am so sad that their bodies are badly burnt, they are hardly recognisable!"

Jo and Mick dragged Pedro and Olive to the Rumble meat fridge, looking up at the lamppost directly outside of the

Rumble fridge with him about to open the door.

Mick looked up at a lamppost, strangely wincing his eyes with the tears slightly affecting his vision. "This lamp post looks a little bit strange; it looks like a soldier is standing at attention with black piercing eyes on a picture card, I think this is terrifyingly creepy!"

Jo looked up at the lamppost again. "Oh, that's creepily odd, I wonder who would put pictures on our near and far lampposts?"

Mick sounded puzzled. "I don't know, we will have a go at washing the soldier picture card off later when we get the steps out of the garage, if that is okay with you?"

Jo agreed. "Yes, we need to keep where we live clean and tidy, I can hear footsteps coming towards us!"

Mick sounded sad, blinking rapidly with his eyes still a little teary, suggesting. "Maybe people have noticed us, and they are coming to say sorry for our loss, what do you think, my eyes are a little blurry, but you are so beautiful, Jo, nobody will ever hurt you because I am your army that will always be in evils way, I will always stop anyone from hurting you while there is breath in my body?"

Witch Sue entered the entrance of the Rumble meat fridge, throwing a potion on Carlos, Pedro, and Olive from her cauldron. "That should do the trick!"

Jo shouted at Witch Sue. "What did you just throw over our children at the entrance of our Rumble meat fridge?"

Witch Sue walked off shouting, and cackling. "They will be with you again, but not as you knew them alive, and you will be joining them soon when they bite you!"

Mick yelled, wiping tears from his eyes. "What does that mean, you are speaking in riddles!"

Witch Sue disappeared from sight.

Carlos, Pedro, and Olive stood up to attention and started to march towards the graveyard with Olive leading the way, with Mick speaking. "We are definitely not taking their bodies into the Rumble meat fridge now because they have come back alive and I think that zombies eat their dinner in the dining room and our neighbour told me the other week that their dog ate some Scrabble pieces, the vet said that the next bowel movements could be spelt out as the word disaster."

Jo laughed, trying to hold her tears back. "Someone told me the other day that pirates don't have a wash before walking the plank because they wash up on shore."

Mick laughed, also trying to hold tears back, rolling his eyes with them walking towards the graveyard. "At least we are trying to cheer ourselves up!"

Jo grabbed Mick with them hiding behind a gravestone, with Jo speaking. "Look, Witch Sue is taking control of people appearing from their graves!'

As they arrived at the graveyard, Witch Sue was speaking to many people with piercing black eyes with spiders walking off the bats' backs. "You are under my spell, now follow me to the graveyard!"

Mick looked puzzled, whispering. "I don't understand how Pedro, Olive and Carlos died, and they are walking about again with other people that look dead, and bats and large black spiders seem to be attracted to them?"

Jo sounded as puzzled whispering. "I agree, what is that blue stone that you were talking about earlier that is in our Rumble meat fridge?"

Mick looked and sounded puzzled, scratching his head, and whispering to Jo. "It was a strange light blue stone that fell from the sky, I put it onto a shelf in our Rumble meat factory fridge to keep it safe!"

Jo repeatedly pointed. "Look, Witch Sue is just there, she looks proud and jolly to be taking control of the victims!"

Witch Sue stood looking over Mick and Jo, interrupting them with a stupid grin on her face, laughing, and replying. "The vampires are my army now and you and Mick are the first to die with my newly woken vampires' teeth because you cannot kill my newly created army because they are already dead and what do you call a group of baby soldiers?"

Mick panicked, biting his nails nervously. "Is the answer by any chance, babies?"

Witch Sue cackled, clapping loudly. "I hope that my claps made you jump, and the answer is an infantry!"

Mick tried to laugh, shaking with his nerves getting the better of him. "Please stop this and turn our lovely children Pedro, Jo and Carlos back to normal right now!"

Chapter Five

Deadly

Witch Sue laughed, announcing. "Don't worry because I have got my torch watch here that will stop you from moving so that my soldiers can kill you both so that you can join me!"

Jo whispered to Mick. "Let's go and hide because we are being chased by dead people and I feel terrified for our lives and that torch watch sounds horrible!"

Mick grabbed a bone from a skeleton's finger that was running past him, Mick poked Witch Sue in the eye with it, and he then shouted to Jo. "Run with me while Witch Sue is distracted messing with her painful eyes making her temporarily blind!"

Mick grabbed Jo's hand with them running off together, hiding behind any gravestones that were available in between the gaps.

Jo sounded terribly upset, breathing heavily. "I can't believe that worked, at least we got away from her for the moment!"

Mick sounded panicky. "Let's travel around here to warn other normal people so that they can stay indoors to keep safe away from the vampires and someone told me that they went to a wedding, and it was beautiful because even the wedding cake was in tiers!"

Jo laughed. "That was a cool joke, and out of curiosity, how many tiers of wedding cake were stacked up?"

Mick laughed. "There were four tiers to the cake!"

Mick and Jo stood behind any walls that they could hide behind, with Mick speaking. "I feel uneasy and like we have got no control; we will observe what is going on from here behind the walls of this house!"

Sue led the army away from the graveyard to kill more people." We will knock on everybody's doors to see how many we can kill using many different random ways!"

Pedro walked into a random person's house with other dead people following him inside. "I am sorry, and I can't apologise enough, but your sheets on your bed are deadly dangerous!"

The victim from the house looked puzzled asking. "Why are my sheets deadly, they look okay and comfy enough to me and you look strange like you have been burnt?"

Pedro wrapped it around their heads with help from the other vampires that had entered the house, with the door being left open. "It looks like we have got a bigger army now because I have strangled them, and they look deathly in the face following me!"

Jo and Mick were stood spying and listening to what was unfolding from behind an alleyway with Jo speaking. "In my opinion, I think that it is something to do with that lamppost that has got a picture of a soldier standing to attention and it reminds me of a man in the shop the other day saying that his least favourite month is March!"

Mick tried to giggle slightly as a tear of sadness rolled down his cheek. "Maybe yes, or it could be something to do with the cauldron attached to Sue's broomstick or the blue stone that has fallen from the sky that is in our Rumble meat fridge and the doctor said to a lady in a shop the other day, urine trouble because you have got kidney stones!"

Jo laughed a little, looking frightened replying. "I think that the lamppost with the soldier on it may be connected yes, and I am just thinking a while ago I was looking up at the sky and a child asked me how most of the stars die, I told the child that it was most probably because they overdosed."

Mick smiled. "I think that they were talking about the stars in the sky and look our daughter Olive is over there walking towards us, I have never seen her eyes look so dark before, they look like they are evil, she must be a vampire!"

Jo looked and sounded distraught. "I know and I wish that we could stop this, these vampires are trying to kill everyone to make more vampires, it is the worst traumatic situation that we have ever been in, let's just secretly follow behind her to see what she does next!"

Olive walked into another person's house. "I am sorry, but I am out of control, and I cannot stop myself from attacking you all with this painting from your lounge walls and I don't feel my normal self!"

Olive bumped into Carlos with Carlos speaking. "I am waiting for the homeowner to answer the door because I quite enjoy shutting people's heads in the cupboard doors because it feels therapeutic in some ways, I can't seem to stop myself from hurting people, I don't really want to do it, it feels so wrong!"

Mick and Jo eventually sneaked over to the Rumble factory without being bitten, with Jo sitting looking at the blue stone from the fridge, speaking. "I have never seen a stone like this before, I think that it is very unique in the way that it sparkles, and I am positive that we need to be patient with geologists because they have all got their faults!"

Mick laughed, commenting. "I think that we need to look inside of Witch Sue's cauldron to see what is inside to see if we can add anything to the potion to stop this happening with more lives lost, and in my opinion, if I were a door, I would be so open to a new situation right now!"

Chapter Six

Cauldron

Jo looked outside of the Rumble fridge door to see if Witch Sue was about speaking. "Witch Sue is near to me, and she has got a great big smug smile on her face stirring her cauldron, I will come inside for now away from her!"

Mick smiled. "I still think that Witch Sue's cauldron has got something to do with all of this!"

Jo smirked. "I agree we need to find a way to look inside of her cauldron, I wish that there was a door that would open up to a better situation, and I will look inside if I ever get a chance if the opportunity ever arrives, and I think that it is the potion inside that is causing all of these problems and I think that a witch that lives on the beach is called a sand witch!"

Mick smiled. "I like that, or it is the torch on Sue's watch face that is making the spell more permanent, because it is powerful enough to make you stop doing something, so it wouldn't surprise me, I am just thinking the other day I ate a clock, it was very time-consuming, especially when I went back for seconds."

Mick chuckled, grabbing the blue stone from the Rumble fridge shelf. "Let's both try to touch the stone together in case it has got some kind of superpower to help us!"

Jo nodded yes. "I doubt it will do anything, but yes, we can do that anyway!"

Mick and Jo sneaked out of the Rumble fridge door, noticing Witch Sue and hid behind her when she was not looking.

Jo laughed silently, whispering. "I will throw some leaves that I have found on the floor into the potion while Witch Sue isn't looking so that it mixes together inside of the cauldron to see if it changes anything for the better, while I am doing this someone said to me the other day that they had got their doctors test results back and they were upset because it said that they were going to be a doctor!"

Mick laughed, whispering. "You are daft, and those leaves have made the situation worse because the people that have come alive, I have noticed that they are getting extra weapons to kill people with as they need them, this is a terrible bloodthirsty life-threatening, dangerous situation and for some reason, the leaves have turned red!"

Jo grabbed Mick's arm, pulling him away with them walking back towards their Rumble fridge, with Jo whispering to Mick. "We need to get back to our Rumble fridge where we will be safe!"

Pedro appeared in front of them. "You do realise that I am going to have to kill you both!"

Pedro had a blank look, with Jo trying to explain. "We are yourselves; Olives and Carlos's parents, please don't kill us!"

Pedro sounded confused. "Who are Carlos and Olive?"

Mick shouted. "Run Jo and save yourself because the evil must have taken over their bodies completely, you don't want to be like my uncle Frank, he wanted his ashes putting in his favourite beer mug, did you know that we call his mug Frank in Stein!"

Jo had a nervous laugh and ran towards the graveyard.

Pedro got distracted by Olive covered in blood at the side of him speaking. "I am trying to enter this house to slit their throats with a knife out of their kitchen draw, I feel bad, but I can't stop myself, it feels like my body has been taken over!"

Mick ran behind Jo towards the graveyard while Pedro was distracted, with him catching Jo up with them hiding behind a gravestone with Mick speaking.

"I feel out of breath, but at least we have escaped for now without being bitten, look, that is frighteningly scary because my name is on the gravestone that we are hiding behind, Carlos mentioned that he had noticed his name on a gravestone, earlier as well, this is so spooky!"

Jo sounded sad. "That is so bad, we need to find a cure fast!"

Witch Sue appeared near to Mick and Sue showing her watch face torch with it glimmering into the cauldron, showing the time with her muttering to herself loudly. "I love being the boss and in control!"

Mick was spying around the gravestone at Witch Sue and noticed Carlo's walking around slowly with black eyes with him pointing at Carlos whispering to Jo. "I will try to get a hair from Carlos's head, but I am not sure how I am going to do it yet and I will then put it into Witch Sue's cauldron to see if that does anything and I can't help thinking about the delusional electrician, the last that I heard about him he was not properly grounded in reality believe it or not!"

Jo laughed silently replying whispering. "We shouldn't really be cracking jokes in this dramatic and traumatic bloody situation, but it is helping me to get through this, look Carlos is over there, I think that we really do need to attempt to drag a hair from his head somehow to see if we can do anything with it that may help us!"

Mick mentioned. "I will have to catch Carlos first because he is running around the graveyard causing havoc with his hat, he is trying it on any dead people to bring them back alive turning them into vampires, this is totally devastating, I think that we will definitely lose the battle, we may as well give up and join them!"

Jo announced her idea. "We can't give in so soon, I will pretend to be dead then steal a hair from Carlos's head, I am laying on the floor in view of Carlos trying to stay still but it isn't easy, they will most probably notice my chest moving up and down as I breathe, because the vampires don't look like they are breathing normally like us!"

Carlos walked over to Jo with him speaking. "You will walk around like me soon when I have bitten you and poured this potion on you!"

Mick walloped Carlos over the head with a spade that he had found, knocking him to the ground with Jo speaking. "I feel relieved that you did that, I have luckily got a hair from Carlos, what do we do now, we need to get away from here before he gets back up?"

Mick suggested. "At least I didn't kill him because he is already dead, I think that you need to put the hair inside of your necklace pendant for now to keep it safe Jo, and this makes him independent around my neck!"

Jo glanced up with her eyes. "You are silly, at least the hair is safe in my pendant now for later, look Olive is here, she looks dreadful, and her black eyes look scary!"

Olive grabbed hold of the hat that Carlos had with her speaking. "I will put it on your heads to take control of you both, whoever puts the hat on your heads controls you!"

Mick yelled. "No, you can't do this to us and control us Olive, this is just not right!"

Olive was trying to put the hat on Jo's head with Jo speaking. "I am going to keep moving out of the way because you are not controlling me like a puppet on a string, this is not right, I am your mother, you should be there to support me, not turn me into a vampire!"

Pedro walked over to Olive with Pedro asking her. "Do you need some help, Olive?"

Olive's evil, shining black eyes shone. "Mother and father, I don't know what is wrong with Pedro because he looks like he is burnt and bloody and my skin doesn't look great either!"

Jo looked at Olive strangely. "Did you hear her Mick she remembered Pedro; she must be in there somewhere still!"

Pedro had an evil laugh announcing to Mick. "If you go past this lamppost, you will automatically turn into a vampire!"

Mick whispered to Jo. "Keep hold of the blue stone with me and let's run to the church to see if we can get inside, with it being a religious place we may be safer!"

Mick and Jo ran over to the church and tried to unsuccessfully open the doors, then hid behind a gravestone with Jo speaking. "I hope that you have got a good idea up your sleeve!"

Mick shook his head no. "I wish I did!"

Chapter Seven

Kiss

Jo cried. "Someone else must have got hold of the hat because more victims are being turned into vampires because everyone around us that has changed has got blood dripping down their lips!"

Mick wiped Jo's eyes. "I will try to remove Sue's broomstick from behind her with her not noticing then she will lose her main weapon, her cauldron that she uses, and I am just thinking that a magician wears a top hat so that the audience can't see his favourite animals, his hare and rabbit."

Jo laughed, explaining her idea. "I don't know if it's a good idea going near to Witch Sue, but we could give it a go, I will pretend to join in being dead wiping blood on my face from this blood-sodden jacket that I have found on the floor so that we blend in hopefully un-noticed, we just need to get inside of the Rumble meat fridges holding the blue stone that will hopefully protect us!"

Mick nodded. "Yes, we will then find out if the blue stone helps us walk past the lamppost and I really hope that we are not turned into vampires, and this bloody situation is getting worse, and do you know that ghosts donate bloody plasma?"

Jo wiped a tear from her eye. "Your jokes get worse!"

Mick agreed, walking behind Jo speaking. "You are as crazy as me with your jokes getting worse, look, we can't go near to Witch Sue because she has got too many spiders, bats and vampires around her, they must be loyal to her now, I heard them discussing where the blue stone had landed so that she could cast a spell to control the whole world, I feel a little nervous in case Witch Sue notices that we have got the blue stone!"

Mick grabbed Jo's hand, with them both holding the blue stone between them slowly walking past the lamppost looking up at the soldier on it with Mick speaking. "We have got past the lamppost, and we have not changed into a vampire yet, that is good!"

Jo smiled. "Let's just get inside of our Rumble meat fridge and lock the door fast!"

Mick pointed at the Rumble meat fridge door. "Quick, run inside and we can lock the door!"

Jo looked in horror from the tiny gap in the letterbox."They have followed us and Carlos is trying his best to put the hat on people's heads, it looks like a blood bath out there with him kissing the ladies, that's not good, and Carlo's is looking at their skirts and trousers like he fancies them, and I am changing the subject for a good reason, at least we know that the blue stone has got some sort of power to stop us being turned into a vampire?"

Mick looked upset, breathing a little too fast. "Yes, that's good but the only problem is that Olive, Pedro and Carlos know where the stone is as well as us so we could be up shit creak without a paddle if we are not careful!"

Jo wiped a tear away from her eye. "Oh no, we are not safe anywhere and did you know that next-doors cat had eaten some yarn the other week and, in the end, it had some mittens?"

Mick laughed, announcing. "I really do think that it is inappropriate for jokes but I need it to help my mental health at the moment and I have got a feeling that we may not survive this because we are in danger, but now that we are locked away in our warm cosy office safe in our Rumble meat fridge hopefully far enough away from the outside world, we can enjoy our last moments enjoying each other's lips with a last loving kiss!"

Jo smiled. "If that is our last kiss and cuddle, it is something to make me smile, it felt like a soft massage on my lips with your lips being so soft."

Mick cuddled Jo speaking. "I love kissing you Jo, it felt like the sun is shining through the clouds with me feeling on top of the world."

Jo sounded panicked. "Someone is knocking on the outside door; I don't think that they are coming in!"

Mick guessed. "It will be the vampires trying to get inside of our Rumble business!"

Chapter Eight

Infected

Jo was hysterical all of a sudden, looking through the letterbox again." Our customer is here to pick up some meat, we cannot open the door because it may be a trap to take the blue stone and then kill us, I feel so stressed right now, please give me another kiss and a cuddle to make me feel better!"

They cuddled for a moment.

Mick started to panic as well, with him kicking the office door in a rage. "Ooh, that hurt, I will not be doing that again and you need to open the door, but you cannot let anyone else inside Jo!"

Jo looked through the letterbox. "Oh no, the customer's eyes are completely black as coal glimmering the same as Olive's eyes earlier, this indicates to me that he is a vampire as well!"

Mick looked sad. "I feel that we can't open the Rumble door because it's too dangerous and I am just thinking that most people think that cobras and rattlesnakes are very dangerous, but really they are completely armless!"

Jo laughed. "We would cry if we didn't laugh, I suppose!"

Witch Sue was standing on the outside of their Rumble door shouting. "You may as well come out because you are going to die both of you, then you can join my team of vampires, it may as well be sooner rather than later!"

Jo whispered to Mick. "Can we crawl through the sewers to see if we can escape to safety that way, I know that it will be a bit smelly, what do you think?"

Mick whispered back. "When we first got the keys to this Rumble meat factory building, I have always wondered where the spooky-looking steps through this door under the factory would take us!"

Jo whispered. "Let's get a knife each then we can go and find out stabbing any vampires that get in our way or try to chop their heads off, but we must keep hold of the stone, I will grab my phone and my waterproof bag, let's go!"

Witch Sue put some potion from her cauldron through Mick and Jo's Rumble letterbox. "You will join us one way or another, you will not escape us!"

Jo shouted back through the letterbox. "The potion doesn't work while we are alive!"

Witch Sue cackled back. "It will wake the dead down the steps, though!"

Mick whispered to Jo. "Ignore her and let's go and get some knives and try to reach safety to hopefully get some help from others that are not infected, it's a shame that we are having to leave our new Rumble home, and I am just thinking, the other day I heard the elderly chimney speaking to the younger chimney saying that he was too young to smoke!"

Jo chuckled. "You are daft, oh no, listen carefully, the vampires are breaking the door down because I can hear the bangs echoing down to us, there must be loads of them by now out there infected, I am just going to write a note on my phone screen saying run and hide to any future victims while we are walking in case we don't make it out alive!"

Mick kept tight hold of the blue stone, putting it into his pocket speaking. "Please follow me Jo, we need all of the luck that we can get and please keep putting your hand in my pocket to make sure that you are touching the blue stone in case we do bump into any vampires down in these sewers!"

Jo agreed. "It is like a secret tunnel, I don't know who has put this here, but it's like it's meant to be here for us to use, and I am just thinking that I read something online the other day about a prisoner digging his way out making a tunnel to a kindergarten, as he arrived he shouted that he was finally free and a child playing next to where he had popped out of the soil shouted, I am four!"

Mick shook his head, looking, and sounding frightened. "We are daft, and I just wish that we had a better light than our phone torches, it isn't really bright enough with it being dark down here, I heard rumours recently from people around here and our customers that there are bodies down here that used to be vampires years ago with all sorts of scary blood thirsty things going on!"

Jo screamed. "The rumours are correct, we need to run past the vampires now because they are trying to grab hold of us, we must have woken them up somehow or Witch Sue has woken them with that potion that she had put through the letterbox!"

Mick was about to be touched by a vampire leaving his coffin. "It's like they can't touch me for some reason; their piercing black eyes make them even more frightening!"

Jo looked at the blue stone." Maybe the stone is like some kind of force field stopping us from getting hurt when holding it, a bit like the lamppost earlier, but I guess when it is used by Witch Sue, it works differently!"

Mick cried. "I don't know what the blue stone is doing but it must be something positive because the vampires and a bat are trying to bite my neck with them being unsuccessful because we are only just outrunning them with the vampires walking slower than us, and the bat and the vampires have got some kind of force field stopping them getting near me and please keep touching the stone with me, Jo!"

Jo agreed. "My thoughts are that I think that it is the stone that is stopping us from being killed and I am just thinking about a newspaper article that I read the other day saying that a child survived a lion attack, so the parents called him Claud!"

Chapter Nine

Hat

Mick had a dodgy fake smile, looking and sounding concerned. "They have caught us up, we are totally surrounded, the vampires are multiplying by the second and freaking me out with their piercing black eyes!"

Jo spoke in a panicked tone. "One of them is trying to put the hat on us, I am so glad that they can't do it because the blue stone must be stopping them with us holding it!"

Mick grabbed the hat. "I can't believe that I could grab hold of the hat, I thought that it was just for people that have turned into vampires to use, this makes me feel more confident and someone told me the other day that hat salesmen drink a cappuccino when they are thirsty!"

Jo suggested, chuckling. "Try putting the hat on one of the vampires' heads and touch them with the stone to see if that does anything, Mick, it is all trial and error!"

Mick agreed. "I am doing that, my god it looks like I have cursed him because he is trying to run away from all of the vampires, and this reminds me of a rumour that I heard the day that a tree tried to run away but someone told him that he wasn't out of the woods yet!"

Jo giggled, pointing out. "Oh dear, it looks like he is re-infected because Pedro has just bitten him that has just been cured on the neck!"

Mick put the hat onto another victim's head. "I have put the blue stone on them as well, but a leaf that is a red colour has just blown onto him and it's like they can't go near to him now, like he is touching the stone!"

Jo looked hopeful. "Yes, this is amazing, we have finally found a cure, I think, by the look of it, it must be a leaf that I threw into the cauldron earlier that has blown down here in the sewers!"

Mick looked happier, winking. "It is good to have something positive to happen for a change, let's hope that the red leaf blows onto all of the vampires!"

Jo looked and sounded a little disappointed. "There are too many vampires for us to cure!"

Mick pointed. "Look, there is a manhole, we just need to climb out of it so that we can get out of here!"

Jo shouted. "Let's lock ourselves away in that car now that we have got out of the manhole so that we can drive away to safety!"

Mick got into the driveway seat, giving Jo the stone and the hat, with her putting the hat inside of her bag with Mick speaking. "Where should we go?"

Jo noticed a person who was behaving oddly like a vampire in the back seat, he was trying to grab the steering wheel reaching over to the front with his mouth opening wide showing his teeth. "Watch out Mick because he is going to bite you, don't forget that you are not touching the blue stone, I will put it on you!"

Mick was bitten before Jo could touch him, crying. "I have got no help at all now, if I let go of the stone, I will be a vampire as well!"

Mick with his black eyes and the man in the back left the car with Witch Sue getting in the passenger seat, with Witch Sue speaking. "I demand that you give me the stone now or you will regret it if you don't!"

Jo ignored Witch Sue driving off. "You can't touch me because I am touching the stone and I am putting it down my bra so that it is always touching me to stop you from touching me and I am warning you that your aggressive, threatening behaviour doesn't scare me!"

Witch Sue cackled. "I have got my broomstick connected to my cauldron, so you will lose!"

Jo replied, shaking with fear. "Do your worst to me, I used to be scared of bumps, but I am getting over it now!"

Witch Sue chuckled slightly, grabbing hold of the steering wheel and speaking. "If I kill you this way, making you crash, I have succeeded in getting my own way so that I can bring you back to life as a vampire if the blue stone falls out of your bra!"

Jo was fighting with Witch Sue driving the car erratically, with Jo shouting. "I have got this deodorant spray that was in the door compartment, now take this in your eyes!"

Jo had blinded Witch Sue. "You have made us crash into the sea now, all of your potion has gone now into the water, so you are well and truly out of luck!"

Witch Sue smiled. "That's good because anybody that goes into the sea will be infected around here, I know that I can't see, but me and my team will still manage to turn you into a vampire using a pair of piercing eyes, with the precious help that I need from my new and old team of vampires that will eventually find me from my broomstick because it throws out secret sounds that only my vampires, bats and spiders can hear!"

Jo looked and sounded in a panic. "I will get out of this situation somehow and just recently I had a stabbing pain in my eye, the doctor suggested that I should remove the spoon from the cup before I drink from it!"

Witch Sue laughed. "You will die now because you will inhale the spell from my cauldron because it will go into the water near you, my bats and spiders are here already, they are always loyal to me and they can go to get vampire help as well by sending my thoughts to the bats and spiders that they can pass on to the vampires as well as being my backup to help me out of certain situations, so I think that it is you that is out of luck!"

Chapter Ten

Follow Me

Jo grabbed hold of her phone, talking to herself. "I will put my phone into my waterproof handbag, I am going now, oh no, the blue stone has fallen from my bra, I will put the blue stone into my bag, and I will also put my bag strap over my head to keep it safe when I change into a vampire so that hopefully someone else will have a chance of survival!"

Witch Sue followed Jo, launching into the sky on her broomstick and grabbing Jo from the seawater. "I can feel the evil forces from you, your eyes will have turned black by now even though I can't see you, so that means that you are a vampire now so you may as well join me in turning the world into a vampire world!"

Jo screamed. "How do you know where you are going because you can't see?"

Witch Sue yelled in Jo's ear. "Luckily for me, the deodorant only blinded me temporarily with the water washing my eyes!"

Jo grunted. "That's not good, that means that you can see, and that reminds me, someone told me the other day that they had bought a grapefruit and pineapple stick deodorant and it said on the instructions to remove the wrapper then shove up the bottom, and they said that it hurt really bad but on the bright side every time that they broke wind it made the room smell fruity!"

Jo and Sue landed on the sand with Witch Sue giggling slightly speaking. "It says that we are in Scarborough in the UK on this poster that I have found on the beach advertising donkey rides, and I like the large amount of people on this beach waiting to be turned into vampires!"

Jo announced aloud, like she was in a trance. "All of your friends and family will die on this Scarborough beach; I will go and kill some more people, and this sand feels lovely under my feet, exfoliating my skin!"

A random man followed Jo and Sue on the sand, shouting. "Please don't go near these strangers because they're insane and I am just randomly thinking that the way that beaches greet others is through a sand shake!"

Jo did not even smirk turning around and knocked the random man that had shouted to the floor with her handbag with him stealing her handbag with him speaking. "You won't do that again because I have got your handbag now, and I was just thinking the other day my cousin said that most boxers are gay because they are always fighting for belts or a purse!"

Jo and Witch Sue walked off to bite and infect other people with what potion was left and the man that had warned people on the beach ran back to his family with Jo's handbag speaking. "I have confiscated this handbag from a random lady so that she didn't hit anyone else with it!"

The wife of the man suggested. "Let's follow her, or maybe not because look, the phone has got a message on the front screen suggesting that whoever finds it must stay away from them and hide!"

The husband and wife ran off with Jo's phone with the wife of the random man from the beach ringing Carlos. "Hello, I don't know if you know but the person that owns this phone has lost the plot, you need to come and get her and her friend who looks like a witch with her feet not visible, that is just not normal!"

Carlos answered on the other side. "Don't worry, we will come and sort you all out, my mum will be okay now because she is one of us!"

The lady sounded puzzled, replying. "That sounds odd what you have just said, I will leave her phone at the Winking Willy's fish and chip shop behind the counter on the corner for you to pick up when you get here, and it is just them that needs sorting out and for some reason, the lady has got black eyes and she is biting people on their necks then throwing something on the victim's that have been bitten!"

Carlos ended the call, shouting to every vampire around him downstairs in the Rumble fridge. "Follow me, we are all going to Scarborough beach because the bats and spiders say that Sue needs help and a random person that rang me on the phone mentioned that Jo's handbag containing her phone will be in the Winking Willy's fish and chip shop waiting for me to pick it up!"

Crowds of vampires with black piercing eyes gathered, biting and killing anyone in their path with Jo and Witch Sue harassing a young couple enjoying a plate of pasta each looking into each other's eyes romantically with Jo speaking. "I am sorry to interrupt, but I am feeling hungry as well!"

The lady eating the pasta offered a piece of garlic bread to Jo, then screamed, staring at Jo's teeth as Jo bit her neck. "I needed your blood, and you will need your partner's blood as well soon because you will be a vampire the same as us!"

The man with her looked in shock, shaking like a leaf. "Why have you done that, we were enjoying a relaxing meal together in this lovely Ask restaurant looking at the sea in between looking at each other?"

Jo looked at him. "Do you want biting as well, because I could do with some more blood?"

The man ran off, with Carlo's walking in, dropping Jo's handbag in front of her. "There you go mum, the blue stone and the phone have fallen out, I have got to go, look after the hat!"

Witch Sue welcomed the vampires arriving. "Welcome Pedro, nobody can stop us now, we will take over the world!"

The blue stone and the hat were on the floor in front of Jo. "These look cool, I am sure that I had a bag like this with a blue stone inside of it before!"

Witch Sue looked upset. "Don't pick the blue stone up or put the hat on!"

Jo announced. "I have already done it with me feeling confused, what am I doing here, I am looking at myself in the mirror, and why have I got blood dripping down my lips, and I feel more back to normal because I remember our neighbour washing his car with his son the other day, I told him to stop being cruel and to use a sponge in the future instead of his son!"

Chapter Eleven

Blood Dripping

Witch Sue chuckled, announcing. "You have done it now; you have changed back to a normal person again!"

The waitress in the Ask restaurant mentioned. "I watched you put the hat on and touch the blue stone, that's all that I can tell you and you look very confused now!"

Olive approached Jo speaking. "You are going to die again!"

Jo shouted. "No, you are wrong because you need this hat on while I touch you with this stone, it is too late, I have done it, you should be cured now!"

Olive changed from being burnt. "How did my body change from being burnt from the iron fire to me turning back to normal before the fire happened and what is Mick, Carlos and Pedro doing and why has everyone got blood dripping down their mouths?"

Jo suggested to Olive. "Just keep hold of the blue stone sharing it with me and we will hopefully stay normal with nobody touching us, we will get everybody else back to their old selves as well and you were a vampire as well drinking blood until five minutes ago!"

Olive grabbed the garlic from the kitchen. "It's hard to believe that I can't remember being like that, I will draw a circle of garlic on the floor, we can see if it stops the vampires from coming near to us while we have a good think about what to do next!"

Jo complimented Olive. "I think that the garlic is working because the vampires can't cross over the garlic, fortunately for us, it is funny, it looks like they're walking into an invisible brick wall!"

Olive looked stressed, twiddling her fingers. "We need to find a better cure fast because there are even more vampires now taking over, biting everyone in sight and hurting people!"

Witch Sue's torch watch fell off her wrist onto the Ask restaurant floor making a light thud noise as it fell without her noticing with Olive whispering to Jo. "Witch Sue has dropped her watch I will go and pick it up without her noticing to see if that helps without anybody turning me back into a vampire and I am just thinking I noticed a skeleton running away earlier because a dog was after its bones!"

Jo laughed, whispering back, suggesting. "Yes, do that, but keep hold of the blue stone while you are doing it to keep yourself safe!"

Olive walked over to Witch Sue in the Ask restaurant with Carlos trying to bite her with Olive speaking. "Carlos, you can try to touch me, but you will lose because I have got the blue stone, and I am just thinking that skeletons don't enjoy candy because they don't have the stomach for it!"

Carlos cackled, laughing uncontrollably. "I am warning you that you can't keep touching that blue stone, you will mess up forgetting it at some point and we will be waiting to bite you or kill you and bring you back alive as one of us!"

Olive focused walking up to Witch Sue picking the torch watch up from the floor with Witch Sue watching her speaking. "Give me that back now, that is my special watch, it is no good to you!"

Olive casually walked back to Jo. "None of you can get me so stop trying because I have told you that I have got hold of the precious blue stone and the watch must do something more than freezing people or you wouldn't want it back so bad, and I feel glad that it isn't damaged apart from the strap looking a little worse for wear and you forgot the word please!"

Jo looked at the torch watch closely, with Witch Sue screaming. "If you don't give me the torch watch back now, I am warning you, you will regret it!"

Olive pointed out the dial that normally changes the time. "I don't think this dial is to change the time, Jo, and it looks like we are in luck because the strap has broken, that must be how it fell from Witch Sue's wrist!"

Jo looked at the torch watch. "It's got a round-shaped dial with a silver star on the inside of the circle!"

Olive suggested. "I volunteer to touch the dial to see if it does anything!"

Jo nodded yes. "I feel like we are guinea pigs trying something out that we don't know what the end result will be!"

Olive pressed the silver star dial in the inner circle of the watch with her finger. "Wow, it's thrown me onto the floor that was powerful like someone has hit me, I feel like it's knocked me for six!"

Jo looked concerned for Olive. "Let me help you up and I bet a ghoul's favourite candy is lemon and slime!"

Witch Sue screeched. "You will kill yourselves anyway, so you may as well give in!"

Olive spoke sternly. "We will never give up even though everyone around us is wanting to kill us and I bet you vampires don't want to eat candy in case tooth decay ruins your teeth!"

Jo suggested. "What if I put different parts of my body on the silver star dial in the inner circle on the torch watch, I will try my elbow because it is my turn now to risk my life!"

Olive warned Jo. "It probably feels like an electric shock, that is the only other way that I can explain it!"

Chapter Twelve

Scared

Jo put her elbow onto the dial. "I think that we had better give up because I have hurt my bottom falling to the floor, and I am just thinking, do you know what music falls to the bottom of the ocean?"

Olive suggested. "I don't know what music falls to the bottom of the ocean, I hope that you are okay, and I will kiss the silver star dial with my lips to see if it does anything!"

Jo looked scared. "The answer is rock music, and you can do that if you feel brave enough to do that, but you may lose some teeth!"

Olive kissed the star dial.

Jo commented. "You look like you are going to be sick, are you okay Olive?"

Olive dropped to the floor. "I feel sweaty, terrible and weak, I have got a horrible faint sensation like I am energy-less!"

Jo sounded sympathetic. "Wow, you are oddly releasing some sort of floating red gas cloud from your mouth that is as red as blood above us, and why are you not talking, Olive?"

Olive was speechless.

Vampires around them got covered in the red cloud from Olive's mouth, they started to change from one extreme trying to kill people to another extreme looking confused, wondering what on earth was going on around them with one speaking. "I have got one hell of a headache; I feel like I need to lie down and why are we in this Ask restaurant?"

Witch Sue started crying. "You are undoing my hard work, but I have still got my broomstick and my cauldron to help me, the watch was one of my main tools to create my new vampire world, I am asking you again, please give me the watch torch back, I am begging you!"

Olive looked like she was in a trance." I am walking around but I do not feel my normal self with this odd red colour gas coming from my mouth, it looks horrible, but it sounds like it is doing some good at last!"

Jo looked and sounded relieved. "I was worried about you; I am so glad that you are okay, at least your eyes aren't black piercing through my head!"

Olive looked tearful. "I feel so relieved that I am still alive!"

Vampires started to bow to Olive like she was the Queen with one speaking. "You are in charge of us now, please tell us what to do?"

Jo happily spoke to Olive. "It's like you are the boss with the vampires wanting to do everything that you ask with less red blood-coloured gas leaving your mouth, and I really do think that vampires are a bloody pain in the neck!"

Olive smiled, looking at the crowd of vampires. "Yes, they definitely cause a bloody pain in the neck, and you need to touch this silver star dial with your mouths, you will then be in charge to ask more people to stop this situation from happening curing everyone!"

One at a time, they all cured more people with an ex-vampire speaking. "I can see more clearly now, and I hope that this never happens again because being a vampire sucks, we are not sucking blood to succeed for the worst anymore, we are succeeding in our goals of ridding vampires from this planet Earth!"

Witch Sue was distraught because she had lost the fight. "I will keep fighting you all to try to get my own way!"

Carlos and Pedro walked into the Ask restaurant with Jo immediately running over to them, making them touch the blue stone with them cuddling Olive and Jo with Pedro speaking. "I am so glad that we are back together looking and behaving normally, we just need to now find Mick, and I am sure that if you cross a vampire and a laptop, they will both fall in love at the first byte!"

Jo laughed, touching Carlos's top. "You and Pedro look back to normal like you were never burnt, I wonder if the house is still burnt, and I like your joke?"

Carlos shrugged his shoulders. "I don't know if our house is still burnt!"

Pedro suggested. "You stay here and relax while I go and find Mick, I will take the blue stone with me so that I will keep safe!"

Jo suggested. "We may be better only letting people kiss the torch watch safe behind the garlic where Witch Sue can't get to us!"

Pedro sounded disappointed. "But the vampires can't walk over the garlic circle so you will have to put your arm through to the outside of the garlic Jo so that they can still change back to normal, then join us behind the garlic as soon as they have changed back to normal and stand with us!"

Before Olive could move the watch into safety, Witch Sue snatched it from her hand. "All of your hard work is undone; I admit that you gave it a good try!"

Jo made more larger garlic circles. "Everyone please, stand behind the garlic circles while we think of a new plan!"

Carlos looked hopeful. "At least some of us are cured for now!"

The waitress walked past, smiling. "I think that we just need a ding dong the witch is dead noise as the shop door opens to celebrate that a few more people are cured!"

Witch Sue snapped with a threatening tone, laughing. "You will not be safe for very long!"

Chapter Thirteen

Losing Battle

Jo smugly replied. "At least we still have got the blue stone and the hat!"

Witch Sue stared at Carlos, speaking abruptly. "Give me the hat and stone back!"

Olive interrupted. "You have got no manners, and we will never give you the blue stone or the hat back now leave us alone, and you know that Pedro has got it at the moment, and did you know that blue stone in Italian is pietra blu?"

Jo looked hopeful. "I hope that Pedro will find Mick and your night school

Italian lessons paid off by the sound of it, Olive!"

Carlos sounded positive. "I agree, it is nice to be able to speak a few words in a different language and I know that Pedro will search everywhere for Mick!"

Jo's phone rang with her getting it out of her bag. "That's good Pedro that you found Mick, but it isn't good that him and his vampire friends are around the Rumble building and in the Rumble meat factory torturing people!"

Pedro questioned Jo. "How is it going in the Ask restaurant, are you winning the battle with your garlic circles?"

Carlos sat down on the floor. "I am going to sit down and think of our next plan while we are safe for the moment in this Ask restaurant!"

Jo sounded like she was going to cry. "Witch Sue has grabbed hold of the torch watch, so we are all in trouble now for the worst but on the upside, we have got the hat and the blue stone, when people touch the stone and when the hat touches people's heads, they are cured completely!"

Pedro sounded down. "I don't know how we are going to solve this mess once and for all, it feels like a losing battle because Witch Sue is crafty and fast thinking on her feet!"

Jo sounded upset. "I don't know how we can solve this either, but the other good thing is when you make a garlic circle to stand in or touch the blue stone it protects you from turning into a vampire and at least garlic bulbs can take their cloves off when they get hot and I bet a vampire takes a bath in the bat room!"

Pedro sounded disappointed, chuckling slightly. "At least you are trying to lighten the mood, it's like a haunted house in the Rumble meat factory here in Sky with so many dead people that have come alive with no colour in their faces or they are even just walking skeletons, I guess that some of them are immortal with the vampires sacrificing normal people for their blood!"

Jo suggested. "Please have a look around to see if there is anything else on the floor that fell from the sky that we have missed!"

Witch Sue interrupted, sounding jolly. "The lampposts will work for me now that I am back in control of my torch watch!"

Olive quizzed witch Sue with a little sarcasm in her voice. "I thought that it was the blue stone that you mainly needed?"

Witch Sue grunted. "It's easier with the light blue stone because my torch watch is more powerful with it!"

Pedro suddenly shouted down the phone. "The lampposts have got the same pictures that are the same as the unique tattoos on people's wrists with them matching, so I guess people with tattoos the same as the lampposts are affected by being turned into vampires, is it the same situation there?"

Olive shouted at Witch Sue. "You keep out of our conversation, stop poking your nose into our business."

Jo looked at people's wrists around the room. "Yes, I never noticed before, you are correct Pedro, all of the vampires have got different tattoos!"

Carlos stood up. "We just need to work out other ways that work better to cure the vampires!"

Pedro announced down the phone. "I have looked on the outside of the Rumble floor, but I can't see anything, oh wait a minute I have found a small dagger with a light blue stone embedded inside of the handle, it just looks like a large jewel the blue stone inside of the dagger handle!"

Carlos laughed at the vampires with their piercing black eyes still trying to reach through the garlic circle, attempting to bite them unsuccessfully. "You will never get to us!"

Witch Sue bragged. "My torch watch, cauldron and broomstick are helping me to change more people into vampires because as the torch watch bounces onto the blue stone eventually over to Pedro's hand in Sky and then it beams onto my broomstick and cauldron, then an innocent unsuspecting person, that person then immediately after turns into a vampire, it is all helping me I just need the light blue stone back now so that it doesn't take as long, I have had enough of this Ask restaurant, I am going to cause more havoc in Whitby in the UK building my vampire army, I am glad that you wasted your precious time!"

Olive muttered under her breath. "I think that you have caused enough trouble, and I am just thinking someone told me that they mentioned to a doctor the other day, they announced that they were addicted to social media and all the doctor could do was apologise for not following them!"

Chapter Fourteen

Dagger

Witch Sue shouted back as she flew off. "I will always be the winner and there will be no social media soon because they will be too busy biting people!"

Carlos shouted to Pedro down the phone. "Please touch the blue stone on the dagger and we will find out if it does anything to help us!"

Pedro agreed with him about to touch the blue stone when a vampire grabbed hold of the dagger biting Pedro's neck with Pedro screaming down the phone as it dropped to the floor. "I am sorry Jo, Olive and Carlos but I will not be able to find Mick because I will be joining him as a vampire in a minute unwillingly because I have just been bitten on my neck, before I turn abnormal, I need to tell you, I love you and did you know that one hat said to the other hat, you go on, and I will go on ahead!"

Jo was upset, screaming down the phone. "No, this is unbelievable, you should have put some garlic around you to stop yourself from being attacked!"

Olive volunteered. "I will take the hat and some garlic with me in your bag, Jo, with me so that I don't get attacked by the vampires on my way to the Rumble factory, it is a shame that Pedro didn't touch the stone in time!"

Jo waved at Olive with Olive speaking. "I will find Pedro's phone in the Rumble factory and ring you as soon as I get there, and I can sprinkle the garlic in a circle if I can cure anybody when there is more than just me that needs to keep safe!"

Jo shouted back as Olive walked off. "Please cure Pedro and Mick first if you do find a cure and I am just thinking the other day an author mentioned that they had written their manuscript on how to cure an itch, it looks like they will have to start from scratch again!"

Olive chuckled, slightly shouting back. "I will do!"

Carlos and Jo sat down on the floor to rest for a while in the Ask restaurant.

After a short while, Jo's phone rang with Olive speaking. "Hello, I have found Pedro's phone on the floor, I have got the blue stone to stop me from getting turned into a vampire now that Pedro must have dropped it on the outside of the Rumble fridge, so I am going into the Rumble factory, please wish me luck!"

Jo replied back. "Please keep hold of the blue stone, the hat, and the garlic!"

Olive shouted. "I will, I can see Mick, Pedro and the dagger, the vampires are crowding around me trying to touch me, I have grabbed the dagger from the vampire, and I have put the stones together, it's like they are trying to connect with large sparks flying around through the air!"

Carlos shouted down the phone. "I hope that you are okay, and don't let the sparks burn you, Olive, and this reminds me of two sticks that went on a date to watch a football match, but there were no sparks because it was a bad match!"

Jo laughed, slightly interrupting. "I am more glad that you aren't getting bitten, please go and try to touch Mick and Pedro with the blue stone and talk some sense into them, and I bet it smells horrible and deathly in the Rumble factory!"

Olive announced. "Witch Sue has appeared in front of me!"

Witch Sue tried to grab hold of Pedro's phone. "Stop talking and give my blue stone and dagger back now, I have poisoned the lampposts with my potion, if anybody goes near to a lamppost between here and Whitby from now, they will turn into a vampire joining me with them having no choice!"

Olive looked at Witch Sue in disgust. "At least you can't get near to me, and you are totally laughable, why would you think that I would give you items back that would put my life at risk, you must think that I was born yesterday!"

Witch Sue looked serious. "I am never going to give up, you don't know how powerful the stone and the dagger are, I have heard good stories from my witch friends, and this is my chance to control the world!"

Olive carried on speaking to Carlos and Jo. "I have just noticed that there is a vampire that has got sparks flying onto his body with them growing larger! "

Witch Sue shouted. "Stop ignoring me, I will keep being in your face until you take some notice of me!"

Mick and Pedro appeared next to Olive with them getting covered in sparks with Olive speaking. "I can't keep hold of these stones anymore because it's putting pressure on my hands making them weak, and it's making me feel like dropping them because it feels like some kind of force field is making them clash and stick nearly together!"

Carlos screamed. "Please, just whatever you do, don't drop them, Olive!"

Olive mentioned. "The vampire ran off that had sparks on him, maybe he has changed back to normal, what do you think Jo or Carlos?"

Witch Sue interrupted. "They will not stay normal for long because I will sort you all out!"

Olive looked angry, in the face. "Just go away and stop interrupting us, you are nothing but trouble, Witch Sue!"

Jo yelled down the phone. "At least we are heading in the correct direction, that's good at least we have started curing people!"

An ex-female vampire wondered up to Olive talking. "I can see clearly now!"

Mick and Pedro stood there looking lost with Pedro speaking. "I am glad that me and you are back to our normal selves Mick, it's such a relief!"

Chapter Fifteen

Garlic Circle

Jo grabbed some garlic from her bag. "I have drawn a circle for you so that you are safe in the middle of the garlic!"

Witch Sue banged her broomstick on the floor in rage. "I have had enough; I am going to make a potion with my cauldron that will hopefully stop the sparks from curing people, because this isn't good!"

Carlos laughed down the phone. "It is good, and I think that you are clutching at straws now, just go somewhere on your broomstick to where you will be able to get lost and stop bugging us, and I had lost 10kg the other day because someone had stolen my dumbbells!"

Olive grunted slightly, blurting out down the phone to Jo and Carlos. "Oh no, there is a cloud that has risen from Witch Sue's cauldron, I just hope that we are safe behind this inner garlic circle, it sounds really bad on both sides of the phone!"

Witch Sue shouted. "Now that the people are under my control that have inhaled my potion in this Rumble factory, you are now my army, and you can all go and get the people that are not affected and infect them by biting them!"

Olive looked at Witch Sue. "You are solidly in control for now with your potion and the lampposts, but we will work this mess out, I have had enough of the red bloody mess on the floor!"

Jo yelled down the phone. "Please bring the dagger and the stone back here to the Ask restaurant with Mick and Pedro and we will see if anything can be done with the hat, dagger and the blue stone!"

Olive agreed. "We will have to leave the rest of the cured people behind the garlic circle, myself, Mick and Pedro, should be okay touching the stones on our way back to you at the Ask restaurant, and how is Carlos?"

Jo looked at Carlos snoring sitting up with him toppling over onto the floor, breaching the garlic line. "Oh no, we are in even more of a troublesome mess now because it looks like Carlos is a vampire now because one has bitten his neck, already dragging him towards them!"

Olive gasped over the phone. "This situation is getting no better because as we are walking past the lampposts, we can see that people are immediately changing into vampires without being bitten on their neck, before we know it, we will be even more surrounded, this is such a sad situation to look at!"

Jo screeched down the phone to Olive. "We have got no chance of survival; I hope that you are nearly back with us!"

Olive sounded upset, with Mick and Pedro muttering to each other in the background. "I am driving a car that I have found with the keys in the ignition, so we are not far away from the Ask restaurant now, Jo!"

Jo sobbed, struggling to speak. "We have even lost Carlo's now, it gets better, then it seems to always take a turn for the worst in anything that seems to get better, you need to stop all of this Witch Sue right now!"

Mick shouted down the phone. "I will give you a big hug in a few minutes when I see you in the Ask restaurant, Jo!"

Pedro yelled at all of the vampires on the way inside of the Ask restaurant. "Put your teeth away and stop trying to bite us because you are not going to get anywhere near to us!"

Mick reached out to Jo as he had crossed the garlic line. "I am so glad that we are back together with Pedro back to normal again as well, it is just a shame that Carlos is not normal anymore, I felt feelingless with nothing in my head when I was a vampire, it's great to feel back to normal!"

Pedro inspected the dagger containing the blue stone. "Now that I feel safer behind this garlic line, I have noticed that it says that we need a hair from a vampire before anyone can be cured!"

Olive laughed. "How are we going to get a hair from a vampire without being bitten, has anybody got any bright ideas up their sleeves to save the world?"

Carlos was joining in, trying to grab into the circle with his hands. "Come out of that circle of garlic and let us bite you!"

Jo started to cry. "We need some kind of miracle to solve this problem!"

Pedro stood looking at the dagger, thinking. "When we are holding the stone and the dagger we cannot get anywhere near the vampires, it is like some kind of force field is stopping us from going near to them protecting us from danger, so it is a case of one of us sticking our arm out risking our lives!"

Mick yelled. "You have got the hair inside of your necklace pendant Jo that was around your neck, where has it gone?"

Jo felt her neck. "I bet it fell off into the car when me and Witch Sue were under the water inside of the car!"

Witch Sue looked up as Jo mentioned her name. "I thought that you didn't want anything to do with me, why did you mention my name?"

Jo angrily answered. "I was just talking about you, and I was definitely not talking to you, so please keep your nose out!"

Pedro looked at Witch Sue volunteering. "Well said, I will come and find the necklace containing the hair with you Jo in the car, the sea water may have moved it!"

Chapter Sixteen

Wind Circles

Jo held the dagger, with Pedro walking off swimming towards the car with Jo speaking. "She annoys me, and we need to keep hold of the dagger because vampires are following us into the water!"

Pedro went down under the water to the car, finding the pendant on the seat trying to speak without swallowing too much water resurfacing, with them just keeping their heads above the water. "Now that I have got the pendant, let's get back to the Ask restaurant as soon as we can so that we are safe behind the garlic circle!"

Jo and Pedro walked back to the Ask restaurant, stepping behind the garlic with Mike speaking. "Myself and the other people around me were so worried about you both, what do we do now?"

Olive suggested. "We could put the hair on the dagger to see if it does anything!"

Mick looked sad. "It hasn't done anything, it was all a waste of time, and did you know that some magazines are sad because they have got too many articles?"

Jo was in deep thought, smiling and suggesting. "We could put the piece of hair on the writing, only on the dagger where it says hair to see if it does anything to start with!"

Pedro put the hair on the writing with a warm wind circling all of the vampires with Olive speaking. "The vampires are all changing back to normal, you can see the puzzled look on their faces, it is like a magical wind, I didn't know that hair could be so powerful!"

Mick pointed out. "The Ask restaurant door has just opened, and it has now shut on its own, I think that the warm wind will cure everyone outside as well, hopefully putting everything back to normal with no more vampires threatening our safety!"

Jo looked surprised. "Yes, everything is going back to how it was before, maybe this is it; we have done it!"

Witch Sue laughed. "You are going to regret doing that because if another blue stone falls from the sky, my torch watch will tell me that it is about to fall!"

Carlos ran towards Jo. "I am so pleased to see you Jo, I think that we need a hug!"

Witch Sue looked upset with her fighting a losing battle with a constant wind coming from the dagger.

Jo announced. "I think that the dagger and blue stone is definitely the key to saving the world!"

Everyone was cured.

The ex-vampires that had been dead a few days came back to life that were dead in the ground before, or the victims that were about to go into the ground had a second chance at living longer and going back home to their families and friends.

One ex-vampire muttered to himself as he walked away. "I can't believe that I am alive again, I will be able to go and see my newborn baby girl for the first time now that I have obviously miraculously recovered from my heart attack somehow!"

Another lady screamed. "I can smell the fresh flowers again; this feeling is as fresh as a daisy!"

The End

Other books by the author Anita Kirk

About the author

Anita Kirk is from Yorkshire in the United Kingdom, she works full time and writes many book genres in her spare time with unlimited talent to write anything, she loves swimming, line dancing, holidays, music, films, writing, reading and spending time with friends and family.

All of Anita Kirk's books
have got <u>funny moments</u>
that may make you feel
like laughing your socks
off.

The Saucy Juicy Pain Game

This is an erotic game that is set in the jungle, with plenty going on to challenge the players, including pain-enhancing needles, animals, and challenges.
Do they survive to the end?

In a Quarter of a second and the Glowing Rings has got two magical action-packed time travel adventures inside.

**<u>Dream Changing</u> is about a lady who can see people's dreams and can change them.
Does Flora help to save the world after visiting the opticians receiving more hassle and drama than she bargained for?**

Sexy Antics is for adults to enjoy; you will never look at a magazine in the same way again.

Magical Footsteps has got a friend that has gone missing that needs finding with help from strangers, with them ending up inside of a game.

Unexpected Jewel has got different stories inside full of mythical creatures, and it is full of magic.

Sexy Shenanigans has got four stories for adults to enjoy with the last story having horror inside as well.

Christmas Sparkles has got fairies inside of this book and a fairytale cottage

where they live, the
fairies need help from
two children and other
people to get people onto
the nice list to save
Christmas, with so much
more inside for you to
enjoy.

Mel's Adventure has got a
story with pictures for
the younger end or
anyone that needs a
simple story to learn the
alphabet, with a song
and a few words in a

different language to
learn as well.

<u>The Sound of Ticking</u> is
about a man who owns a
shop in New York and
receives a telescope for
his birthday, his life is
soon turned upside down
with unpredictable
challenging situations
taking him to many
places in time to solve
many mysteries.

Wings to Heaven. This is a true story about my dad's life before, during and after dementia and Alzheimer's.

Sexy Revenge is for adults only, it's about a man that has a car accident, and his life is stolen by his best friend while he's in a coma, does Jenson kick some ass getting his own back?

<u>Fun Dance Book One</u> has got many dances to follow by yourself or with others, it is ideal for any age.

<u>Spooky Scary</u> needs garlic circles and so much more to bring people back to normal everyday life with many obstacles and drama along the way.

TIME TRAVEL LIP BALM

Enjoy the adventure, the lip balm dramas inside of this book are very unpredictable and fun, it's full of jokes and lighthearted entertainment for anyone to enjoy from adults to children.

These books have been written so far with many more available soon.

Remember that you can follow and contact Anita Kirk with any questions or comments on Tick Tock, Facebook, Twitter, LinkedIn or you can email any comments to anitajane1@outlook.com Please contact Anita if you would like a shop opening or anything else and she will get back to you as soon as possible with an answer.
If you have enjoyed reading Anita Kirk's books a

good review would be appreciated and if you could share Anita's books on your social media, and with your family and friends she would really appreciate your help.

Thank you for your support in reading this book.

All of Anita Kirk's books are available on Amazon and some other online shops.

*<u>A good review would mean a
lot if you have enjoyed
this book.
Thank you in advance for
your good positive review
it is very much
appreciated.</u>*

**Thank you again**

PLEASE TYPE ANITA KIRK INTO AMAZON

FOR ALL AVAILABLE PUBLISHED BOOKS

OF MANY DIFFERENT GENRES.

__Erotically Spooky__ is the same as __Spooky Scary__ but it has got a little bit of raunch, and vampires attempt to take over the world with funny moments to make you laugh out loud.

__Thank you.__

Twitter – Anita Kirk, author @AnitaKi73550337

LinkedIn- Author Anita Kirk

Instagram-

<u>Please don't forget to leave a good review if you have enjoyed reading this book and share it with others on social media or in person.</u>

<u>Thank you again.</u>

@anitakirkauthor

<u>You can also follow Anita Kirk on tick tock.</u>

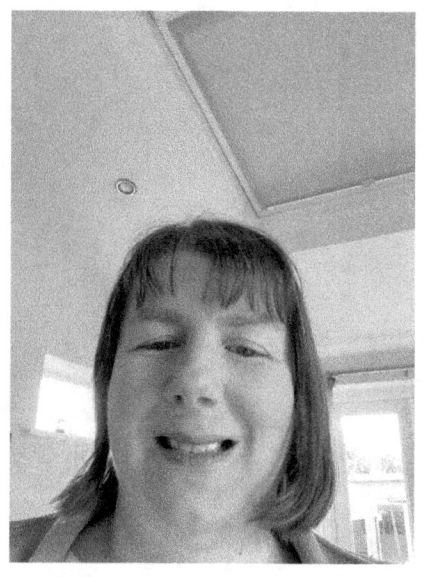